CIVIL WAR BREAKOUT

Great Escapes
Nazi Prison Camp Escape
Journey to Freedom, 1838

GREAT ESCAPES

CIVIL WAR BREAKOUT

BY **W. N. BROWN**

EDITED BY **MICHAEL TEITELBAUM**

HARPER

An Imprint of HarperCollinsPublishers

ISBN 978-0-06-286042-2 (trade bdg.)

ISBN 978-0-06-286041-5 (pbk.)

Typography by David Curtis

20 21 22 23 24   PC/BRR   10 9 8 7 6 5 4 3 2 1

❖

First Edition

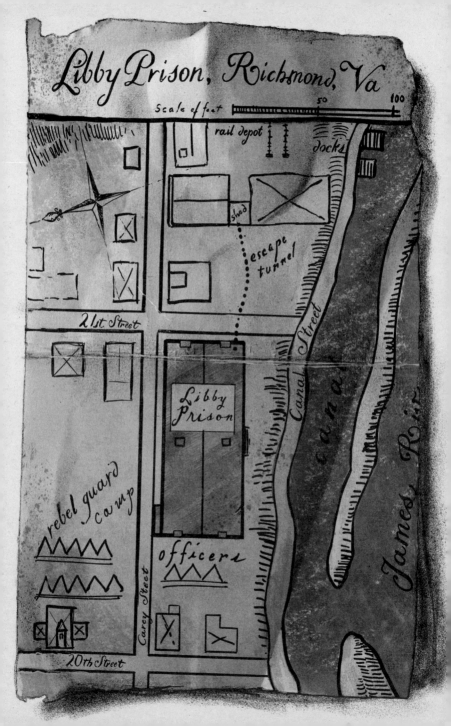

Chapter One

THE NEW ARRIVAL

"Yankees, keep it moving!"

On a sweltering-hot September afternoon in 1863, Union colonel Thomas Rose swatted away mosquitoes as he shuffled down the dusty Richmond, Virginia, street. He was one in a long, slow-moving line of captured Union soldiers. Dehydrated and exhausted, the soldiers struggled to keep upright as Confederate guards on horseback barked orders. Yet despite his parched throat and sore, bleeding feet, Rose managed to hold his head high and keep pace with his horse-riding enemy. He refused to let the Confederates, or "Rebels," as he thought of them, see him suffer. Ahead of him in line, a younger officer stumbled and nearly collapsed.

If we don't get some water soon, Rose thought, his black hair and beard dripping with sweat, *we're all gonna keel over . . .*

Rose didn't know where the Confederates were taking the seventy Union soldiers they'd captured. He and his fellow Northerners had come all the way from Chickamauga, Georgia, where they'd been taken prisoner by the Confederates and herded into overcrowded cattle cars. It had taken two days to reach Richmond by train, making stops along the way in South and North Carolina, where they were insulted and spat on by the local townsfolk. The men were given some water but no food, and there was no room to sit or lie down.

Now as Rose marched in the suffocating Virginia heat, his belly ached from hunger.

"Halt!" a Confederate yelled. The prisoners stopped in their tracks.

Rose raised his eyes to peer through a steamy haze of kicked-up dust. Ahead of him, an enormous three-story brick building loomed—Libby Prison.

It looks more like a warehouse than a prison, Rose thought.

Built on the outskirts of town, a few yards from the James River, the monstrous edifice with barred windows was to be his home for the foreseeable future. He realized that if it were this hot outside, inside wouldn't be any cooler. Rose shuddered, knowing that once they entered the prison, some of his fellow soldiers—and even Rose himself—might never leave.

Thunderheads rumbled in the distance, the dark clouds rolling across the sky like advancing cavalry.

As Rose watched, two Confederate officers rode their horses over from the prison stables.

Surely that man riding in front isn't in charge of the prison, Rose thought. *He doesn't look a day over twenty-five.*

"Welcome home, boys," the young man shouted in a thick southern accent from atop his horse. He was sharply dressed in a gray Confederate frock coat, its polished gold buttons almost blinding in the sun. A commanding officer's hat shaded a narrow, clean-shaven face. To Rose, he almost seemed like a kid playing dress-up in his father's clothes. "My name's Major Thomas Turner. I'm

the commander of this prison. My second-in-command is the old boy to my right, Warden Dick Turner—no relation."

Rose glanced over at the commander's underling. Unlike his boyish-looking superior officer, the older Warden Turner had a scarred face and a yellow, rotten-toothed grin. He held a bullwhip in his right hand.

"Y'all mind the rules, and we'll get along fine," Major Thomas Turner continued. "Step out of line, you'll wish you were dead. See, ol' Dick here used to run a plantation, so he knows how to run a tight ship."

Around Rose, a few of the other prisoners shuffled uneasily. He knew they were thinking of the reports they had heard of the brutal conditions of Southern slave plantations, and the cruel nature of plantation overseers. Rose was a Northerner who believed that slavery must be abolished. Although many of his fellow Northerners were indifferent about the plights of enslaved people in the South, Rose was proud to lay his life on the line in honor of his belief. He wasn't alone: if the newspapers were to be believed, more than two million Northerners of all backgrounds had joined the fight to end slavery and keep the country together. At the same time, about a million Confederates were fighting to hold on to their states' legal rights to own human beings as property. They believed that if slavery ended, there would be no one to work the plantations and their economy would collapse.

BLACK AMERICANS IN THE CIVIL WAR

Americans of all backgrounds and ethnicities fought in the Civil War. Although exact numbers are unknown, at least 180,000 free black men fought for the Union Army. Some had formerly been enslaved, and some volunteered from as far away as Canada and the Caribbean. By the end of the war, 40,000 black soldiers had given their lives fighting for the right of all black people to be free.

Rose watched as Warden Dick Turner, in his gray Confederate uniform, kicked a prisoner who was muttering under his breath. The prisoner fell to the ground.

"No talking!" Warden Turner screamed.

While some others helped the prisoner back to his feet, Major Thomas Turner continued.

"There'll be a head count every morning after reveille. Chow time is twice a day. My rules are simple: keep in line, do your time, and you live. Step out of line or try to escape—you die." He paused and smiled. "Now y'all enjoy your stay."

He nodded to one of the guards, who bellowed, "Inside, now!"

The prisoners began shuffling toward two massive wooden doors. Rose peered up at the towering building. Through the barred windows, he could see the ghostly shadows of the inmates moving around inside.

Once through the doors, a wave of damp heat and rancid air hit Rose like a punch in the face. The young officer who'd nearly collapsed during the march finally toppled over the moment he stepped foot in the building. He lay in a crumpled, convulsing heap on the wood-planked floor. Rose winced as the man began vomiting.

"Get that lazy Yank to his feet," the guard barked.

Rose gritted his teeth and helped peel the young officer off the floor.

"Stick these boys on the second floor in the lower Chickamauga Room," one of the guards told another, nodding toward a group of prisoners that included Rose. "And put the rest on the third floor. And somebody get this boy up—Lord almighty, what a mess . . ."

Rose followed the other prisoners up the creaking wooden staircase. Emerging on the second floor, he grimaced at the sight of the Libby inmates already there. Many were rail-thin and looked as if a strong breeze could knock them over. Yankee uniforms hung loosely from their skeletal frames. Their beards and hair were wild and unkempt but did little to hide drawn cheeks and sunken eyes. The air was stifling, the stink of a hundred or more unwashed men packed into one room almost unbearable.

How can a man last in this place? Rose thought.

He made his way into the room. There were no cots or blankets for cold nights. Here the prisoners had almost nothing, just a couple of crates and makeshift benches cobbled together from spare wood.

"Welcome to the Chickamauga Room," one of the guards drawled. "Figured it'd be the most appropriate place to stick you fellers since that's where y'all were captured."

"I feel at home already," Rose replied without missing a beat.

The guard laughed in return and left the new prisoners to find a bit of floor in the crowded room.

As Rose looked around, a crack of thunder shook the walls, followed by a collective groan in the room. Some of the men scrambled to their feet, seeming panicked, while the new arrivals looked on, confused.

Rain began to pour. As Rose watched the deluge outside the four small, barred windows, he realized he couldn't ignore his scratchy, bone-dry throat a second longer.

"Pardon me, sir, where might I get some water?" he asked a prisoner standing next to him. The man was wearing a major's uniform.

"In that washroom yonder," the major said.

He took his measure of Rose, then handed the colonel a metal cup.

Rose thanked him and headed over to the small room. There was a large sink and trough with a legion of flies buzzing around it. The colonel turned the faucet and filled the cup with brackish river water. He had barely wetted his gullet and stuck the cup back under the spigot for a refill when he heard a commotion coming from the first floor.

What's going on down there? he thought, glancing at the stairwell.

Then he felt something crawling on his arm. Looking back, he saw a giant rat on his sleeve.

"AAH!"

Rose ran out of the room, with the soaked, screeching rat clinging to his uniform. Before the creature could take a bite out of his neck, Rose reached up, grabbed hold of the squirming animal, and threw it to the ground. He watched in disgust as it scurried away. As he looked back into the washroom, to his horror he saw dozens of rats climbing out of the drain in the trough and through holes in the wall. They emerged from every opening—the windows, the stairwell, and each hole, crack, and cranny in the walls and floorboards.

One older, particularly crazed-looking prisoner with a white beard laughed.

"Say hello to the welcome wagon, fellas!" he cackled.

Rose watched in awe as the prisoners knocked the seemingly fearless rodents off their trouser legs in an almost comical dance.

Looking around, he spied the major who had given him the cup calmly observing the scene from his corner. Approaching him, Rose handed the cup back and asked, "What is going on here?"

The major grinned and shook his head. "I should've warned you about the rats. Happens every time it rains. They climb up through the walls to escape the flooding river water. Better get used to it, 'cause it rains quite a bit."

Kicking what had to have been a three-pound rat off his boot, Rose turned to the window and stared out at the river and beyond. *This is no prison*, he thought. *It's the seventh circle of hell. And I'll be damned if I'm going to rot in here!*

Chapter Two

THE OLD FIREPLACE

After two weeks at Libby Prison, Colonel Rose decided to head downstairs to the prison kitchen to see if he could find some extra food. He could handle the lice that seemed to thrive in his unwashed Yankee uniform—the bites almost drove him mad the first week, but now they were just an annoyance. The severe lack of food, however, was another thing.

The vermin and filth I can take, he thought, *but I can't handle the starving!*

The kitchen was the only ground-floor room in Libby Prison that inmates were allowed to freely enter and leave during the day. Otherwise they had to stay upstairs on the top two floors. The kitchen had two rusted stoves, where prisoners who were appointed cooks prepared food the Confederate guards provided. Often the food was barely edible, but the prisoners still lined up to get as much as they could. If a scrap fell to the floor, it wouldn't stay there long—the rats made sure of that.

Rose made his way over to one of the stoves, hoping to find an uneaten morsel.

He was so intent on scrounging for food, he didn't notice the tall, thin prisoner leaning against the wall across the room.

"Hungry, Colonel?" the man asked.

Rose looked over his shoulder and saw the major he'd spoken to on his first day in the prison.

The major held out his hand and offered Rose half a roll.

"Much obliged," Rose said, taking the hard roll and biting into it hungrily. "Seems I'm in your debt again."

The major laughed. "Don't worry about it. It

takes a while to get used to the ration system down here." He extended a hand. "I'm Major Andrew G. Hamilton."

"Thomas Rose, colonel. Pleasure to make your acquaintance."

"Where you from, Colonel?" Hamilton asked. "You have a familiar accent."

"Pennsylvania."

"Me too," said the major. "That is, before I moved to Kentucky."

They spoke briefly about their mutual home state.

"I was captured in northeast Tennessee," Hamilton said. "Ran into a Reb cavalry up in the Appalachians. How about you?"

"Chickamauga, Georgia," Rose replied.

Hamilton whistled. "I heard about that battle. One of the bloodiest fights of the war so far."

Rose nodded, and as he spoke of the battle, Hamilton saw that the older man wasn't afraid to take chances.

I bet this fellow wants to get out of this hole just as much as I do, he thought.

"I'll be honest, Colonel," Hamilton said. "I've been watching you the past few days, studying the windows, the walls, the fireplaces. . . . Seems you also spend a lot of time looking at that large sewer to the south of the prison. I believe you're thinking about the same thing I am."

"Oh? What would that be?" Rose replied.

"Getting out of here," Hamilton said with a grin. "And I think I know just where to start."

"Where's that?"

"The east cellar," Hamilton said. "It used to be the kitchen before they began cooking in the luxurious quarters you now find yourself in. The cellar floods easily, and the Rebs got tired of it. Well, that and all the rats. I've heard some of the guards affectionately call it Rat Hell."

The colonel shuddered. If the rest of Libby were any indication, he'd hate to see what the guards considered a really bad rat infestation.

"They closed the stairwell entrance and locked it up pretty good," Hamilton continued. "But I reckon we can find a way in. From there, we'd have to dig a tunnel through the wall to the sewer. It would be risky and a lot of work, but I think it can be done."

Rose paused to think about Hamilton's plan. *Tunnel out of the cellar?* He had to admit, it was a better idea than anything he'd thought of so far. And after all, Hamilton had been in Libby much longer than Rose and knew the layout of the place.

"All right," Rose said. "But how do we get down there?"

The major nodded toward the two large stoves. Then he leaned closer to Rose. "Behind those stoves," he whispered, "lies an old fireplace. Behind the fireplace, the adjoining chimney connects with the cellar below."

"Ah." Rose nodded. "So we remove the bricks, and climb down the chimney."

Hamilton slapped his new friend on the shoulder. "Nothing gets by you, Colonel," he said with a wide smile.

Rose laughed. At least Libby hadn't taken away his new friend's sense of humor.

A TYPICAL DAY AT LIBBY PRISON

Libby Prison was a three-story tobacco factory that became a prison in 1862 to hold Union officers captured during the war. Each floor had three rooms. Most of the prisoners lived on the top two floors. The first floor had an office for prison officials, a kitchen, and a hospital. The cellar had a cooking area, a space where black prisoners were housed, a dungeon used to punish prisoners, and a workshop.

Prisoners were awakened at the break of day. After a head count, they were told to wash up. Using the bathroom was something prisoners dreaded. Each washroom had a single trough into which more than a hundred men had to relieve themselves. The stench was horrible, as many prisoners had diarrhea from the bad food. Flies and cockroaches were everywhere. The men washed up with brown river water piped into a sink. The rare prisoner who had a toothbrush could brush his teeth with the river water.

Prisoners ate two meals a day—one at noon and

another at dusk. The ones who volunteered to cook were given food by the guards, usually bacon, beef, beans, rice, or corn bread. The cooks would do their best to give every man an equal portion, which usually didn't add up to a lot. As more prisoners arrived, food became even scarcer, and the men had to survive on rotten rations covered in bugs.

Often the meat was spoiled, moldy, and full of maggots. Black bugs covered the beans and corn bread like poppy seeds on a roll.

One thing the men looked forward to was opening packages sent from home. Prisoners in both Union and Confederate prisons were allowed to receive packages from loved ones, mostly containing much-needed food and clothes. However, Warden Dick Turner and his guards went through each package and took most of the food. Whatever was left over was given to the prisoners. Sometimes Major Turner would revoke this privilege after a prisoner had broken one of the rules, which would upset inmates, who often depended on those supplies for survival.

Higher-ranking officers among the prisoners were allowed to get shaved and have their hair cut by barbers. As the war went on (and the Confederacy lost money), this privilege was revoked.

With nothing to do all day, the men had to entertain themselves. They would play cards or chess with soup bones as the playing pieces. Others would hold political debates or stage fake trials over imaginary property. Some would carve names, song lyrics, or poetry into the prison's wooden beams. Lice-racing was another popular activity. Lice were placed on a plate, and the prisoners would bet on which one would run off the edge first.

Prisoners who were wounded or ill were cared for in the first-floor infirmary. Patients lay on filthy mattresses crawling with lice. Medical tools weren't often sterilized, and the smell of gangrenous, rotting flesh was enough to make even the most hardened soldier retch. If prisoners were unlucky enough to find themselves in this room, they usually never left alive.

Lights-out was at nine p.m. Without any blankets, men without coats were left to shiver on the floor during the winter. In the summer, whatever breeze came through the windows offered little relief from the sweltering heat. Prisoners would sweat and scratch at lice all night long, getting what little sleep they could.

Outside the prison, twenty-five to thirty guards patrolled the grounds nonstop, day and night. They were ordered to shoot any prisoner who came within three feet of a window. The outside of the first floor was painted white, so anyone trying to escape would be seen more easily. Any guard allowing a prisoner to escape could be sent to jail.

Chapter Three

RATS IN THE CELLAR

Rose and Hamilton spent the better part of October and all of November examining their escape plan from every angle. They memorized the guards' schedules, and Rose learned the prison layout. They both knew that if they were caught, they could be whipped, locked in the prison dungeon, or shot dead, so they wanted to be extra sure the route they chose was their safest option.

"The way I figure it," Rose said, "your original idea of tunneling out of the east cellar is still our best chance." It was a cold December morning, and he could see his breath as they huddled together in the back of the Chickamauga Room.

"The west cellar is out because the guards sleep right above it. Digging from the middle cellar's out, too, because that's where the dungeon is . . ."

Libby's so-called "dungeon" was the cold, dark place where rule breakers and prisoners who were disfavored were held in isolation with no light, barely any room to move, and only bread and water to eat, often for weeks at a time. The poor souls locked away there often had to catch and eat rats just to survive.

Hamilton nodded. "It's time we started. I'll head down there tonight. You stay up here. That way, if I get caught and sent to the dungeon, one of us is still around to work on the tunnel." Rose reluctantly nodded his agreement. "Be careful."

That night, while everyone else was asleep, Major Hamilton got to his feet in the darkness and crept down to the kitchen. The wooden stairs creaked with every step, and he waited at the bottom of them with bated breath for a guard to come and investigate.

When none came, he quickly moved over to the two stoves. By the light of the moon streaming through the barred windows, the major slowly and quietly moved one of the stoves aside, revealing a fireplace. He removed the ashes and took from his pocket a knife he'd borrowed from a friend. Then Hamilton knelt down and began the slow and tedious work of chiseling out the mortar between the bricks at the back of the fireplace. Sweat ran down his forehead, from both the effort and the fear of being caught. Every time he thought he heard a guard walking past the kitchen window, he stopped chiseling and lay flat on the floor. Only after the guard passed would he resume. After two hours, he'd managed to dislodge only three bricks.

This is harder than I expected . . .

Finally, after another hour, he removed enough bricks to feel a draft of air through the chimney behind the wall. Hamilton set his knife down. With sore hands, he replaced the bricks and put the stove back into place.

That's enough for tonight, he thought as he snuck back upstairs. *My hands can't take any more.*

The next night the work began again. This

time Rose insisted on helping his friend. After following Hamilton to the kitchen and pushing aside the stove, Rose crouched in the fireplace and took up the pocketknife, ready to do some chiseling of his own. The colonel attacked the mortar, working fervently.

The two continued to trade off chiseling duties over the next nine evenings, with Hamilton working one night and Rose the next. Christmas came and went, barely acknowledged in the prison.

Finally, on the evening of December 30, Hamilton was able to remove enough bricks to stick his head and shoulders through the fireplace wall and look down into the adjoining chimney.

This is it, he thought. He peered straight down the narrow, soot-covered shaft. Beneath him, the shaft curved around and dropped into the east cellar a few feet down. He could smell the cold, dank air of the open space below.

Abandon hope, all ye who enter here, Hamilton thought, remembering the famous line from the *Divine Comedy*.

He paused a moment, contemplating whether or

not to go and wake Rose, before trying to squeeze his body into the chimney.

What if I get stuck and can't get out? he thought. *The guards would see the removed stoves and the bricks and I'd be caught for sure!*

Hamilton steeled his nerves. After all his hard work, his excitement to test the tunnel was too strong to ignore. With any last-minute doubts shaken off, Hamilton climbed into the hole, lowering himself down feet first. The chimney was cramped and snaked a bit on the descent. He had to slide in on the floor as he entered the small passage, then push himself straight down, and then again to the right.

I sure hope this will be large enough for Rose to get through, he thought, imagining his friend's six-foot-two frame.

After wriggling himself through the final bend in the shaft, Hamilton, now covered in soot, felt his legs kick out into open space. He dropped down about four feet onto a floor cushioned with straw. The east cellar was blacker than night, the air as cold as a cave. He also heard an all too familiar noise—the scratching and skittering of Libby's permanent rat residents.

Hello again, my four-legged friends, he thought.

Hamilton struck a match and saw the straw moving with hundreds of screeching rats, climbing over one other to escape this new intruder. Some of the rats were almost the size of small dogs, the largest he'd ever seen.

Dear Lord, now I know why they call it Rat Hell.

Hamilton clenched his fist and started forward slowly so as not to blow out the match light. His face contorted at the odor of the cellar, a horrible mixture of spoiled pork fat and rat droppings.

At the far end of the room he could make out the east wall. He walked over and ran a hand along the damp stone and mortar.

Seems older than the fireplace construction, he thought. *Hopefully it's more penetrable. . . .*

When he turned around to head back, the match blew out.

Hamilton grimaced.

That was my last match!

He hurried across the moving floor. Then a

familiar squeal rang out under his feet. Hamilton winced, realizing he'd stepped on one of the rats. Gathering his courage to continue, he felt his way along the wall until he was able to find the small passage opening that led back to the first floor. He jumped and pulled himself up into the chimney, banging his head on the top of the brick entrance in the process. After climbing back out into the kitchen, Hamilton rubbed the knot on his head and breathed a sigh of relief.

If I'm gonna tunnel out of Rat Hell, he thought, *I'll have to get less squeamish . . . and bring more matches!*

He quickly and quietly replaced the bricks and pushed the stove back into place. Then he crept back upstairs to the Chickamauga Room. He found Rose sleeping in his usual spot in the corner.

"Rose!" he whispered.

"Yeah?" the colonel answered groggily.

"I did it! I broke through to the cellar!"

"Well done, Hamilton," Rose said, rubbing his eyes. "Now get some sleep. Tomorrow's going to be a long night."

Chapter Four

EXCAVATION BEGINS

Around midnight the next evening, minutes before the first day of the new year, Rose followed Hamilton down to the kitchen. Together they removed the stove, and Hamilton showed Rose his work, taking out the loosened bricks in the fireplace and exposing the entrance to the tunnel.

"Now, it's a little tricky getting through," the major told Rose. "You've got to—"

"I can manage," the colonel cut him off. "See you down there."

Facing the floor, Rose awkwardly climbed into the hole feet first, sucking in his gut and squeezing down as far as he could go. At that moment, Hamilton heard a Confederate guard stop outside the window. He could also hear the colonel struggling in the chimney.

"Help!" Rose whispered. "I'm stuck!"

Rose couldn't move his arms at all. He was trapped in the curve of the passageway. Worse yet, his back was bent at a horrible angle in the tunnel.

"Hamilton, I can't breathe!"

Rose's mind raced. *He can't hear me. I'm doomed! God help me, I'm going to die in the chimney of Libby Prison . . .*

Hamilton's face suddenly appeared in the darkness above.

"Quiet!" he hissed. "There's a guard outside!"

"Help me," Rose whispered between gasps.

Leaning headfirst into the fireplace, the major tried his hardest to pull his panicking friend out of the crawl space, but Rose wouldn't budge. Hamilton knew they had to be as quiet as possible so as not to alert the guard standing outside by the window. Grabbing Rose by the armpits, he tried again to pull him out, but to no avail.

I can't get enough leverage, Hamilton thought. *I need someone to hold my legs.*

"Don't panic. I'm going to go and find some help."

Rose wheezed in protest, but the major was gone.

After silently creeping out of the kitchen, Hamilton scrambled upstairs. He had to find someone he could trust, someone he knew could keep a secret. He had a few friends he believed were up to the job, but they were going to be hard to find among the dozens of men sleeping on the dark floor. With Rose struggling downstairs, Hamilton had to take a chance and settle on a stranger. He knelt down next to an officer sleeping near the stairwell and shook him awake.

"Sorry to wake you, soldier," he whispered. "I'm Major Hamilton, and I need your help."

Dazed, the young man squinted in the darkness.

"With what? And what hour is it?"

"I'll tell you later. What's your name?"

"Lieutenant Bennett," he said, "of the Eighteenth Regulars."

"Well, Lieutenant Bennett of the Eighteenth

Regulars—follow me."

Upon returning to the kitchen, Hamilton was dismayed to see the guard still standing by the window. He put a finger to his lips and led the confused Lieutenant Bennett to the wall with the tunnel and crouched down.

"You need to help me get my friend out," Hamilton whispered. "He's stuck in the chimney. Hold my legs while I pull his arms."

Bennett obliged, holding Hamilton's legs by the ankles as the major bent down into the chimney. Hamilton grabbed Rose under the armpits, and— with the new leverage from Bennett—managed to wrench Rose free just as the guard standing outside the window walked away.

By the time the two men had pulled him out, the colonel was coughing up a storm.

"What are you boys doing messing around down in the fireplace?" Bennett asked with a knowing grin.

"I'll inform you soon enough," Hamilton replied. "We're much obliged for your aid, especially the colonel here. And if you don't mind, let's keep this among the three of us."

Rose noticed Bennett pause, as if he was going to ask another question. Then the young officer seemed to change his mind.

"Yes, sir," he said and crept back upstairs to the sleeping quarters in the Chickamauga Room.

"The passage is a little tight, don't you think?" Rose asked.

"I'll work on it," Hamilton promised. "Why don't you try again after that? Maybe tomorrow night."

"No time. We need to start digging tonight."

"Are you sure? You almost died!"

Rose was shaken up. His large hands were still trembling.

"It has to be tonight," he said. "There's no time to waste, now that we've opened the wall. It could get discovered anytime."

"Okay," Hamilton whispered. "But I don't know if that Bennett kid will want to come down here to save your skin twice in one night."

Hamilton took up the pocketknife and chiseled at the edges of the tunnel where Rose had gotten stuck. After an hour of work, the major felt certain the passage was now wide enough for Rose to get through.

Rose returned to the fireplace, this time sliding in on his back. He managed to curve his body through the chimney's winding passageway and, after about a minute, found himself breathing the rank air of the east cellar.

"I made it!" he whispered up the tunnel to Hamilton.

He lit a match and started making his way over the sea of straw and vermin to the far wall.

Hamilton wasn't lying about the rats, Rose thought. *They're everywhere!*

On paper, their plan seemed simple—breach the wall at the southeast corner of the cellar, then tunnel south toward the main sewer. The sewer pipe opened up into the nearby Lynchburg Canal—and the road to freedom.

Having just climbed down through the chimney after Rose, Hamilton walked over to his friend.

"That's where you want to start digging?" he asked.

"It's as good a place as any," Rose said, feeling

around the wall with his hands.

Hamilton handed the colonel his knife. Rose kneeled down and began chiseling at the mortar between the stones, a skill he'd grown adept at the past few nights. Hamilton stood watch as Rose worked. A candle he'd brought from upstairs flickered in his hand, painting the small cellar room with orange light.

From the hay-covered floor, an eerie sea of glowing red eyes curiously watched these new visitors.

Hamilton grinned. "Never thought I'd be celebrating New Year's Eve in a cellar with a bunch of rats."

"One thing's for sure," Rose replied. "I'm not spending 1864 in Libby Prison."

Chapter Five

PUTTING TOGETHER A TEAM

They returned the next night with two knives and a chisel Hamilton had lifted from the carpentry shop. Over the next several days, they carefully liberated enough stones from the foundation wall to reach the packed earth behind it.

Soon Rose was tunneling into the earth. Scraping away on his belly, he suddenly noticed he was struggling to breathe. *The air is thin underground*, he thought.

Then all at once, a large clump of dirt came loose and rained down around him.

The tunnel was caving in!

"Rose?" Hamilton whispered. He could see Rose's boots sticking out of the crumbled wall.

Kicking and twisting, Rose pulled himself out of the dirt pile. He was covered in soil, coughing and spitting out clumps.

"We need to come up with a better system," he said, wiping the grime out of his eyes. "Next time I may not be so lucky."

"If it caves in once, it will happen again," Hamilton said. "The soil's too loose here."

When they returned the next night, Rose and Hamilton chose another part of the cellar wall. They set to work digging. As the week went on, they developed a routine: Hamilton would stand at the mouth of the tunnel, fanning in fresh air with a hat and holding the candle, while Rose dug. Hamilton also held a rope that was tied to Rose's foot so he could help pull the colonel out in case of another cave-in.

Hamilton was impressed with Rose's tunneling skills. The colonel dug like a man possessed, burrowing through the ground like a gopher.

"You sure you haven't done this before?" Hamilton asked. "You can dig tirelessly for hours without stopping."

"I used to be a schoolteacher," Rose said.

"Compared to dealing with a roomful of rowdy kids, digging out of prison is nothing."

Lying on his stomach in the dark tunnel one night, Rose scraped at the dirt with his knife. His hand grew sore, so he pocketed the blade and began clawing at the dirt with blood-caked fingers. He did this in darkness—the farther into the tunnel he went, the harder it was to keep a candle lit. Deep in the earth, the air was thin, and he struggled to breathe while he worked.

I hope I don't pass out, he thought hazily.

As Rose dug, Hamilton fanned air into the tunnel from the east cellar. Every so often, he felt a tug on the rope tied to his wrist. He would then set the fan down and began pulling on the line. Out would come a spittoon (a pot into which people spat chewing tobacco juice) that Rose had swiped from one of the upper levels. It'd be filled with dirt. Hamilton would dump the dirt onto the floor in a corner, then cover the dirt with straw and return the spittoon to the tunnel.

Eventually, Rose emerged from the tunnel.

Hamilton could see the sweat dripping off the colonel's face in the candlelight as he gasped for air.

"I've been doing some thinking," Hamilton said. "I believe we should look into bringing in more men. It's almost impossible to handle all these tasks while watching and listening for guards."

Rose nodded. Keeping a lookout was important. Though the stairwell entrance to the cellar was locked up, all it would take was for one curious sentinel to walk into the kitchen, see the stove had been moved, and unlock the door to investigate. In that event, Rose and Hamilton would quickly snuff out their candles, lie on the ground in the darkness, and pray they weren't seen.

"You might be right," Rose told his friend. "We could use more diggers too. I thought we'd be further along by now."

Hamilton looked down at Rose's gnarled, bleeding hands.

"No two ways about it," he said. "We need help."

Despite being in a prison full of starving

soldiers desperate to escape, choosing a team that Hamilton and Rose could trust wouldn't be easy.

"We have to be careful about who we bring in," Hamilton warned. "I've heard tell of guards occasionally posing as prisoners, keeping their eyes and ears open, hoping to catch word of any escape plans."

Rose looked surprised. "Really?"

Hamilton shrugged. "I wouldn't put it past them."

"In any event," Rose continued, "that can be avoided. We know Lieutenant Bennett is a good man. He helped save my hide when I was stuck. We'll eliminate the men we don't know."

"If only it were that simple," Hamilton replied. "There've been a few cases where prisoners have snitched on men plotting escape. In exchange for their betrayal, Turner traded their toady hides back to the Union."

Rose was dismayed, but he didn't find this hard to believe. The North and South would sometimes trade their prisoners. Major Turner decided who would be traded and sent home and who stayed to rot. Libby was such a horrible place that Rose almost couldn't blame the Yankees who betrayed their fellow prisoners . . . almost.

Despite the potential danger of betrayal, if the escape were going to be a success, they'd need some extra workers.

"One of the men ratting us out to Turner is a chance we're going to have to take," Rose said.

Out of the four hundred prisoners cramped into the Chickamauga Room, Rose and Hamilton eventually settled on thirteen new recruits by mid-January.

Anxious to escape, the men immediately agreed to help.

"I was wondering why you boys took so long to ask," Lieutenant Bennett told Rose.

With their team assembled, that night, Rose and Hamilton led the new recruits down to the kitchen and through the secret passageway. Once they were in the east cellar, he could see the look of horror on the thirteen men's faces in the flickering candlelight. The rank air combined with the hundreds of rats was a lot for anyone to take. Libby Prison was a house of horrors, but the cellar made the upper rooms look like a fancy New York hotel.

"The walls," Captain Isaac Johnson, a young man from Kentucky, muttered. "They're *moving*."

"Get used to it," Hamilton said. "Welcome to Rat Hell, fellas."

After showing the newcomers the tunnel, Rose explained how things would go. They'd split up into three teams, working in shifts. One team would work on the tunnel one night, while another team would take over the next night. This way, no one got exhausted.

"Because make no mistake," Rose told them, "by the end of the night, you will be *very* tired. Each of you will have a job—one will dig while another fans air into the tunnel. One will hide the dirt under the straw while another stands guard. One more of you will be waiting to take over when a digger gets worn out. With enough hard work, I know we'll make it to the sewer and then to freedom."

"Only at a place like Libby," Hamilton noted, "would a man be thrilled about the prospect of entering a sewer."

The next morning, Bennett approached Rose in the Chickamauga Room.

"I knew it was going to be a challenge," Bennett said. "But I must admit I had no idea."

The colonel grinned as Bennett described the previous night's misadventures. He and another recruit, Major B. B. McDonald, had been among the first of the new team chosen to dig.

"Rats were crawling up my pant legs," Bennett recounted. "Major McDonald almost lost it after his turn digging. One of the squealing vermin had crawled out of its hole into the tunnel and scratched his face. McDonald scrambled out, sweating and cursing. Thankfully, we were able to calm him down before he got too loud."

"Well, it shouldn't be long now," Rose said. "If my calculations are correct, we'll hit the sewer sometime next week."

Bennett ran a dirt-encrusted hand through his hair.

"I sure hope so," he said.

Captain Johnson approached Hamilton with a disappointed look on his face. The new recruits had worked well together, and the team had made a lot of progress over the past week without a hitch—until now.

"We've got a big problem, Major," Johnson said. "While we were digging we ran into some of the wooden posts supporting the prison. There's no way we can carve through them with our tools. The wood's got to be almost a foot thick. Half of the men are ready to quit."

Hamilton scratched his beard. "Don't quit yet," the major replied, giving him a pat on the shoulder. "Let us take a look."

That night, Hamilton and Rose crept down into the basement. As Hamilton fanned air, Rose went into the tunnel. It wasn't long before he ran into the large, wooden, dirt-covered posts. He attempted to dig around them on both sides, only to find more posts running parallel and close together. Removing a knife from his pocket, Rose began furiously cutting at the wood. After an hour and many splinters, he had hardly put a dent in one post.

Exhausted, he turned and went back up.

"The war will be over by the time we cut through those posts," he told Hamilton.

The major shivered and pulled his coat around him.

"I don't know if I'll be able to survive another winter in this place," he said.

As a colonel, Rose knew better than anyone that, among soldiers, once disillusionment set in, it could be hard to shake. While he thought about what to do next, Bennett walked over and crouched next to them.

"I think this could help," he said, revealing a pocketknife. The sharp edge of the blade had tiny nicks in it, like a saw. "Using the blade of one of the other knives, I've managed to carve teeth into this one. It could help with the timbers."

Rose grinned. "Bennett, you're a genius. I'll saw some teeth into another knife as well."

That evening, Rose climbed into the tunnel. When he got to the timbers, he began cutting with the newly modified knife. The blade immediately started sawing into the wood.

It's working!

After a few hours, Rose had cut halfway through one of the posts. His hand was sore and splintered, so he was happy to let one of the other men take over. This process would repeat itself over the next two nights. The work was painstaking, but eventually the men were able to cut all the way through the timbers.

With the posts no longer an issue, the dig continued to progress smoothly. Until one night, when Rose was digging through the clay with his hands, he began to feel cold water seeping through the ground.

That's odd . . . I didn't think we were that close to the river.

At first it wasn't much, but after a few minutes he noticed that his trousers were completely soaked. Then, after removing a particularly large clump of dirt, freezing river water began pouring in through the roof of the tunnel!

The tunnel quickly filled with mud and river water, leaving Rose no time to take a breath before he was submerged.

Rose desperately jerked his leg in an effort to shake the rope attached—his signal to the man outside that he was in trouble. But more mud was piling on top of him in the darkness. Soon he couldn't move his leg anymore.

So this is how it ends for me, Rose thought, as the darkness and mud enveloped him. *Drowning in a filthy, rat-infested underground tomb in a POW prison!*

Chapter Six

THE SEWER

Desperate for air, Rose swallowed the filthy water. The sludge caught in his throat. Panicking, he tried to move his limbs, to no avail.

I'm going to die!

Then, after what seemed like an eternity, he sensed the rope around his ankle tighten. As his body was pulled out of the tunnel, Rose felt the weight of the earth around him lessen. Before he knew it, he was back in the east cellar, lying on his stomach and throwing up what seemed like gallons of brown water. The others crowded around him.

"Good God, man!" Bennett said, still holding

the rope. "How much water and mud did you swallow?"

Finally, Rose wiped his mouth and sat up, his bloodshot eyes glowing like two red embers in the candlelight. Bennett wrapped his coat around Rose, who was soaked and shaking violently in the cold.

"Th-that's t-twice you've saved me now, B-Bennett," he stammered.

"You must have nine lives, Colonel," Bennett said. "Looks like we got a little too close to the river."

"This t-tunnel is d-done for," Rose wheezed, "We've g-got to start a new . . . one."

Despite the setback, Rose and Hamilton soon began work on the next tunnel—one that hopefully wouldn't cave in or get flooded.

After studying the prison grounds, Rose had observed that there was a smaller sewer that led to the larger pipeline. This other sewer pipe was close to the east cellar and, if they could crack into it, they could crawl through the pipe and escape through the main sewer.

"All we've got to do is chisel into that smaller pipeline," Rose told the men.

They were huddled in a far corner of the Chickamauga Room, speaking in hushed tones. It was cold and snowing outside. Thin from the lack of food, the prisoners shivered violently in the late January chill. They only had their tattered uniform jackets for warmth, and these were dirty and lice-infested.

LICE!

Imagine you're a young cadet who's recently joined the Union army. You've only been in the field for a few weeks. You're tired, filthy, and scared. You've been marching for what seems like days without a proper wash. Then one day, you begin itching under your wool uniform. Only a little at first, but the itching gets worse as the day goes on. By nighttime, it's unbearable. At camp, by the light of the fire, you peel your sleeves back. Your arms are covered in red bite marks. A grizzled veteran looks at your arms and gives a knowing smile.

"Looks like the graybacks found ya, son!" he says.

Lice were common in both armies during the Civil War. These tiny pests, called "graybacks" by the Union soldiers, thrived in humidity and unwashed wool. They fed on human blood, and could jump from one person to another. Fun fact: by World War I, lice were also called "cooties."

In addition to causing the horrible itching, some of the parasites were carriers of deadly diseases, such as typhoid. Two-thirds of the estimated 660,000 soldiers who died in the Civil War passed away from disease, typhoid fever being chief among them. Signs of typhoid included diarrhea, fever, and overall tiredness. Men with typhoid could often be seen lying around with a dazed look in their eyes. Despite efforts to stave off the disease by enforcing cleaner conditions in encampments, the fatality rate for typhoid was approximately sixty percent by the time the war ended.

"We're with you, Major," McDonald said through chattering teeth. "Let's do it."

Hamilton nodded. He knew the men were tired—tired of spending their nights in the dark. Tired of pawing through the earth like animals, of lying on their backs and stomachs underground . . . But they weren't ready to give up, at least not yet.

"Good," Rose said. "And I think I know how to make things go faster. We'll work around the clock."

"What do you mean?" Bennett asked.

"Exactly what I said. Instead of just working at night, we'll work during the day as well. One team at night, and then another can sneak down into the cellar in the mid-afternoon, before the cooks come in to start making dinner. If no one's around, a team will climb through the fireplace while another man stays to move the stove back in place. The Rebs only count heads in the morning, so we should be able to work undisturbed."

"That's a great idea," Hamilton said. "No one's in the kitchen except for during the two meal times anyways. The more we work, the sooner we can get out of here."

"Dangerous, but worth the risk," Bennett agreed. "Let's do it."

The others noticed Rose knock on the wooden floor for luck as they quickly dispersed.

"We'd better find a way out soon," Hamilton said when he and Rose were alone. "I don't know how many more holes these boys are gonna be willing to dig."

The colonel nodded solemnly.

"Hopefully," he said, "as many as it takes."

A few days later, Rose was resting in the Chick-amauga Room after a particularly grueling shift digging in the cellar, when he was awoken by a weary and smelly—Bennett. The lieutenant told him that they'd reached the sewer pipe, but there was a problem.

"We can't saw through the wood lining the pipe," Bennett said. "It's oak and as hard as petrified wood. It's impossible!"

"Keep your voice down," Rose hissed, covering his nose from the smell. "My God, what have you been crawling in?"

"Sewage is seeping out into the tunnel," Bennett replied. "The stench is unbearable."

"I'll take a look," Rose told Bennett.

Rose made his way to the basement. The smell coming out of the tunnel was indeed horrible. It was so bad, in fact, that the man fanning air into the tunnel had to cover his nose with the frayed collar of his uniform. Rose did the same, and it did little to block the toxic odor.

A few seconds later, Hamilton emerged from the mouth of the tunnel. Even in the candlelight, there was no mistaking how covered in filth he was—except this time it wasn't the usual dirt and mud.

"Tarnation." He gasped. "The stench . . . It's as if it were released from the bowels of the devil himself."

Rose helped him out of the tunnel.

"Were you able to get into the sewer line?" he asked.

Hamilton flicked the excrement off his hands in disgust.

"No, sir," he said. "It's impossible to chisel into it with our tools, and the ungodly slime leaking out . . . It can't be done. Even if we managed to carve a hole big enough, I believe the pipe is too small for a man to crawl through."

Before giving up on yet another tunnel, the colonel had to see for himself. He entered the tunnel and the smell hit him like a cannonball. The rank sewage had already leaked out far into the tunnel, and it wasn't long before Rose was crawling through it. By the time he reached the pipe, its foul contents had soaked through his threadbare uniform.

In the darkness he felt around the wood lining of the pipe and found the place where the others had been cutting. He continued carving in the same area, but the knife kept slipping from his sewage-soaked hands. The stink was overwhelming, and he could barely breathe. Finally, after the knife he was using snapped in two, he gave up and crawled back out.

"Any luck?" Hamilton asked.

Rose shook his head, sending droplets of sludge flying into the air. "Unfortunately, no. I'll tell the others. But first, let's get as much of this foulness off of us as we can. We smell like a saloon outhouse."

Chapter Seven

AN UNEXPECTED ALLY

The sewage turned out to be the breaking point for most of the men. Even Lieutenant Bennett, whose enthusiasm had been unwavering, seemed to be at the end of his rope.

"I just can't do it, sir," he told Rose. "I can't go back into those tunnels. I'm sore all over. I can't take the air, the filth, the rats . . . I'm done."

Hamilton looked at the shivering group of men who were once again huddled in a corner of the Chickamauga Room. They had been digging for weeks. Their tired eyes stared at the floor. Dried, cracked lips and sickly pale skin made them look more like upright corpses than living men.

Feeling deflated, the major was about to walk away when Rose spoke up.

"Gentlemen," he said. "I know you're tired. I know your bodies ache and your spirits seem broken. But we're close. Hamilton and I have been checking the layout of the grounds from the windows, and have figured out a new angle. This next tunnel will be our way out. I give you my word. And if I'm wrong, then quit. No questions asked. Let's all take tonight to rest, and then commence further discussion on the matter tomorrow."

The men groaned in unison, then hesitantly agreed to Rose's terms.

After the group separated, Hamilton turned to Rose.

"I don't recall having any such discussion about a new tunnel," he said.

Rose smiled. "I know. Perhaps we should have one now."

Moving to a barred window, Rose pointed to a shed about fifty feet away from the east cellar. It stood between two larger buildings on the other side of a wooden fence that bordered Canal Street.

"I think we should try to tunnel into that shed," he told Hamilton, his breath steaming in the cold January air.

Hamilton nodded thoughtfully. "It's farther from the river, so the ground will be dry and won't flood. It's also distant from the rest of the prison, so we won't have to worry about hitting any foundation posts."

Later that day, at another meeting in the Chickamauga Room, the two men ran their plan by the others. It took a bit of convincing, but eventually everyone was on board with this final attempt to escape.

Digging on the new tunnel began that night. Although the men were still tired, once they'd managed to chisel through the wall, they found the soil easier to dig through this time around. It didn't take long for them to get farther than they had with any of the other tunnels. This did a lot to lift their spirits.

February arrived. One afternoon, as Hamilton lay on the floor exhausted after a long night, he was approached by a young man named Robert

Ford. Ford was an officer and one of Libby's twenty black prisoners, who slept in the west cellar. Before getting captured, he'd been a teamster for the Union—a soldier who drove a team of horses (or oxen) to transport ammunition and other supplies for the war effort.

At Libby, Ford had been given a job as Turner's hostler, the person who took care of the horses. Hamilton knew Ford was allowed to freely roam the grounds outside the prison walls during the day.

"Are you Major Hamilton?" Ford asked.

"You guessed right, friend."

"Name's Robert Ford."

The two shook hands.

"How can I be of service to you?" Hamilton asked.

"It's I who can help you," Ford countered. "One of your associates approached me with the knowledge of your recent activities. I'd like to assist you in any way that I can."

Hamilton felt he could trust Ford. There were rumors that Ford had helped previous escapees and that he knew a Union sympathizer in the area, a woman named Elizabeth Van Lew, who offered her home as a safe house for prisoners to hide. Some inmates said that Ford was in contact with Van Lew and that he had given previous escapees directions to her house.

"We're attempting to tunnel into a shed on the other side of the fence, to the east," Hamilton told Ford. "I think we're close, but we don't know exactly how far it is."

"The tobacco shed." Ford nodded. "It's between the James River Towing Company and Kerr's warehouse. I'll see what I can do." He lowered his voice to a whisper. "I know a benefactor who might be of service to prisoners once they've vacated this fine establishment. She has maps of safe routes going north."

Hamilton's eyes lit up. Maps with a list of safe houses—places where Union sympathizers hid escaped soldiers or people on the run from slavery—would be crucial to the men trying to make it back to the North.

He was about to ask Ford for more details when

the doors flung open and Warden Dick Turner stormed in. The former plantation manager had six guards with him. He also had his whip in his hand.

Hamilton's gut twisted. He knew this was trouble.

"All y'all line up for a head count," he barked.

As the prisoners lined up, Turner looked right at Ford.

"Get back to work," he growled.

Ford shot Hamilton a look, then retreated down the stairs.

Rose and Bennett walked over to where Hamilton stood.

"It's a surprise head count," Rose said. "Thank God we all decided to take the afternoon off!"

"Not true, major," Bennett said. "Johnson and McDonald are in the cellar!"

"What?"

Bennett nodded, his eyes full of worry. "They said they weren't tired, so I went to the kitchen with them about an hour ago. After they crawled down to the cellar, I pushed the stove back."

This isn't good, Rose thought, biting his lip.

"I said line up!" Turner screamed.

One of the guards began the head count. After he finished, he approached the warden.

"We're missing two, boss."

"Do it again, you idiot."

Rose's mind raced as the guard started counting a second time.

The count's going to be short. We're going to get caught.

Then he felt someone brush against him. He turned and saw Bennett slipping back in line after being counted. He soon noticed Hamilton doing the same thing.

Brilliant, Rose thought with relief. *Now why didn't I think of that?*

The sickly prisoners did all seem to look alike, and their scruffy beards made it even harder to tell one from the other. Turner didn't notice the ruse. This time the count came up to the right number. The escape plan was saved . . . this time.

THE STORY OF
ELIZABETH VAN LEW

One of the most famous Richmond locals who helped Libby prisoners escape was Elizabeth Van Lew.

Van Lew's father had a number of enslaved people in his household; the exact number is unknown. Growing up, Elizabeth Van Lew begged her father repeatedly to free them, but to no avail. Even after he died in 1843, his will had a stipulation forbidding his heirs to free the slaves. So, starting in 1860, Elizabeth paid them wages instead.

As tensions built between the North and South, Van Lew hoped Virginia would side with the Union. Of course, this didn't happen. Worse still, her hometown, Richmond, became the capital of the Confederacy! Despite this, she knew she couldn't stand by and do nothing. She got permission to bring food to Union prisoners held at Libby. To keep in good graces with the guards, she would bring them treats such as baked goods.

When the war broke out, Richmond's citizens

were shocked that Van Lew would dare help the enemy, but she didn't care. She was in contact with a Union sympathizer on the prison staff, and when prisoners escaped, sometimes she would hide them in a secret room in her attic. After word got out to Union leaders that a local woman in Richmond was helping prisoners, the North officially made her a Union spy.

Van Lew would receive messages from Union sympathizers who worked in high offices of the Confederacy. She would smuggle these secret messages out of Richmond to where the Union army was stationed. Oftentimes these messages—which may have contained battle plans or supply shipment information—were hidden in a false-bottom plate warmer, and sometimes even in empty eggshells!

After the war ended, Van Lew was even less popular in Richmond than she had been before. She was also poor, having spent her entire inheritance purchasing the freedom of enslaved people in the area and helping the Union. At one point, she asked the United States government for money to live on. They said no, though President (and former Union general) Ulysses S. Grant did make her postmaster of Richmond during his term as president. Unfortunately, this job ended when Grant's term was over. Van Lew spent her last years as a recluse, living off money sent to her from the grateful families of former Libby prisoners she'd helped. After she died in 1900, the family of one of these prisoners erected a granite headstone in her honor in Richmond's Shockoe Hill Cemetery.

Chapter Eight

THE FINAL TUNNEL

Cold sweat beaded Rose's face as he and Hamilton descended into the cellar on the night of February 8. Despite having made this trip dozens of times over the past month, the threat of getting caught by Turner had made this part of his shift the most nerve-wracking. Once safely in the cellar, he and Hamilton were met by Johnson. He seemed badly shaken.

"Had a close call this afternoon, Colonel," Johnson said. "Bennett was digging and I was on fan duty. Suddenly I heard the rats squealing something awful. Someone was fooling with the locks of the cellar door, so I got down as low as I could and burrowed down under the straw. Sure enough, two guards came through the door at the top of the stairwell!"

His voice began to quiver as he recounted the next part. "They just stood around, mumbling something. I did my best to lie still. I could feel the rodents crawling all over me. It took all I had not to scream and jump up when I felt one crawling across my face. Then, all of a sudden, they left."

"I think we can finish the tunnel tonight," Hamilton assured him. "Robert Ford told me he measured out the distance to the shed with twine. It's roughly fifty-seven feet, and we're nearly there."

As Hamilton spoke with Johnson, Rose went to inspect the tunnel. He crawled downward for the first ten feet before hitting a tight spot. The narrow passage was only about sixteen inches wide, and Rose had to twist his body and inch forward like a caterpillar to get through. This was the part he hated the most, remembering how he'd been stuck in the chimney.

After squeezing through the tight spot, Rose scurried up a slope. He got to the end and began digging with even more intensity than usual. His body ached and his fingers were bleeding (he even lost a fingernail), but he kept going.

Sometime around midnight he felt fresh air on his hands. Dirt fell to the cave floor. His eyes already adjusted to the darkness, Rose could see the wooden ceiling above the tunnel entrance. He was inside the shed!

Slowly, he climbed out of the hole. This was the first time he'd been out of Libby Prison in five months, and he relished the near-freedom. He went to the door of the shed and listened for voices or footsteps. He heard no one on the other side, so he opened it.

He was inside the James River Towing Company office. It was empty. He crept through the building and headed for the door. After listening for a moment, he slowly cracked it open.

Easy does it, he thought. *A creaky door right now could be bad news . . .*

Rose looked out at Canal Street—and it was also empty! Not a Confederate in sight. He let the fresh night air wash over him for a few more seconds. Never had the colonel appreciated a clear night sky as he did at that moment. Then he closed the door and retreated back into the tunnel.

At last, he thought as he crawled underground, *our digging days are over. I can't wait to tell the others!*

"What are we waiting for?" Hamilton said upon hearing the news. "Let's get out of here!"

Rose had just returned from his journey to the outside. The tunnellers were huddled in a corner of the Chickamauga Room.

"I agree," Rose said. "The guards are beginning to get suspicious. I say we leave tonight."

The other men looked at each other. They seemed hesitant.

Finally, Bennett spoke up. "It's four o'clock in the morning. If we make a run for it now, that's only gonna give us three hours before daybreak."

"Bennett's right," McDonald said. "It's not enough time. We're going to need as big a head start as we can get if we're going to make it to Williamsburg—God willing."

Although they didn't like to wait any longer than necessary, Rose and Hamilton knew the men were right. It wouldn't take long for the guards to figure out that so many men were missing. The Rebs would be combing the area on horseback. The escapees would be on foot, and rather than heading directly north, where there would be more Confederate patrols, they would be walking fifty miles southeast to the Union army lines at Williamsburg.

No, the men would need the entire night to get a big enough head start.

"Then it's settled," Rose said. "We leave tonight, just after dark."

The next day, February 9, was excruciating for Rose. He was terrified that the tunnel would be discovered mere hours before they could put it to use.

All it would take is for someone to walk into the tobacco shed and accidentally step into the hole, he kept thinking to himself. *Or unlock the door to the cellar and find Johnson . . .*

Each hour ticked by slower than a snail crawling through molasses. Rose and Hamilton spent most of the day milling around, looking for any signs that the guards were rooting around the cellar.

While speaking with Bennett off in a corner, Hamilton was visited by Robert Ford, who was carrying a large box. He sat it down and opened the top. Inside were horse stable supplies.

"Brought some things that might help you boys," he said. Ford moved aside the supplies and lifted off a wooden panel, revealing a treasure trove of civilian jackets and hats.

"I went ahead and put some maps in a few of the pockets," Ford said.

Hamilton placed a hand on Ford's shoulder.

"I can't thank you enough, Robert. Why don't you come with us?"

"Well, for one thing, I can't quite as easily sneak into the kitchen from where I sleep," he said.

Hamilton frowned. He had forgotten that Ford and the other black prisoners of war slept in another part of the prison, the west cellar.

"We're locked in for the night," Ford continued. "Also, I'd be the first one Turner noticed went missing since I work the stables for him, and they'd catch on about the escape much faster. Don't worry about me, though. I'm just waiting for the right opportunity."

The major nodded.

"We're grateful for your help," he said. "I'm in your debt."

The men shook hands, then Hamilton and Bennett removed the clothes. Ford placed the wooden panel with the stable supplies back in the box and picked it up.

"Godspeed, boys," he said. Then he turned and hastily left the room.

Suddenly a commotion broke out as the door to the Chickamauga Room swung open. In walked the sneering Major Thomas Turner, flanked by his second-in-command, Warden Dick Turner, and a few guards. The prisoners eyed the twenty-one-year-old Confederate and his cronies with burning hatred.

"Now listen here," Major Turner barked. "As I'm sure all you blue jackets know, five of y'all done escaped our lovely facility."

Rose and Hamilton gave each other a glance. They'd heard rumors that morning that some men had managed to disguise themselves as guards and walk out of prison, right through the front door. Word had it the uniforms had been smuggled to them by a local Union sympathizer.

"That's right," Major Turner continued. "Some more foolish Yanks took it upon themselves to leave a little early. But don't y'all worry, 'cause they'll be back. And I'm gonna personally put them in the deepest, darkest dungeon I can find."

Warden Dick Turner kicked a small makeshift bench out from under one of the prisoners, grinning as the older man fell to the floor in a heap. Libby's second-in-command was known for his sudden outbursts of violence, often targeting the sick, old, or weak.

"Now, I would just as soon shoot the whole lot of ya myself right here and now," Major Turner said. "But that wouldn't be civilized. So there's gonna be a few changes around here. No man here is allowed to leave this room. No more wandering in the stairwells, the halls, or down to the kitchen unless it's chow time. You got me?

"Good. And just so you know I ain't foolin', my second-in-command, Dick Turner— "

"No relation," the prisoners said in unison. They knew this routine all too well.

"Right." Major Turner's young face twisted in a smile. "He's gonna personally shoot any man caught messin' around where he ain't supposed to be."

Warden Dick Turner looked directly at Rose and Hamilton. He grinned, his teeth yellow and mossy.

"Shoot ya down like a dog," he said.

Then the Confederates left the room.

Rose swallowed hard. He thought about his wife and children. The fate of the other tunnellers ran through his mind as well. Was his plan going to get them all killed?

He turned back to the other men. Before he could open his mouth, McDonald spoke.

"It'll take a lot more than Turner's threats to keep me from getting out of here!"

The others nodded in agreement.

Rose was glad to hear it.

Finally, darkness came.

The crew waited until ten o'clock. They had decided that every tunneller could choose one friend to take along. With the number of escapees now rising to thirty, Rose and Hamilton decided that leaving in shifts would be best. The last thing they wanted was a stampede of prisoners rushing to escape. That could only end in disaster.

Rose crept slowly down the stairs, Hamilton close behind him. He peered around the corner into the kitchen. His heart leaped in his throat when he saw a Rebel soldier, looking bored and smoking a cigarette.

There's a guard standing against the stove!

Chapter Nine

THE SHED AT THE END OF THE TUNNEL

Rose turned immediately and began motioning the men back to the Chickamauga Room.

Upon hearing the news of the Confederate guarding the kitchen, the other men's faces fell. The tunnellers and some of their friends were dressed in the civilian coats and hats Ford had given them, anxious to leave.

"Turner's beat us," McDonald said. "We're never getting out of here!"

"We're not licked yet," Rose said. "I'll check the kitchen again in an hour."

The minutes slowly ticked by. After about an

hour had passed, Rose crept once again down the stairwell. He looked around the corner.

The kitchen is empty!

He waved his hand, encouraging the others to follow.

Rose, dressed in a brown coat and gray hat, tiptoed over to the fireplace, his head darting back and forth, searching for guards. He and Hamilton then slowly moved the stove for the last time.

Before entering the chimney, the two men shook hands. They had been through a lot together.

"Been an honor," Rose whispered.

Hamilton smiled. "See you on the outside."

The colonel crawled into the fireplace passageway. Maneuvering the tight, twisting space was as easy as slipping on a comfortable pair of shoes now. Rose wondered how the other prisoners, who hadn't been through the tunnel yet, would fare. It would be a challenge, to say the least.

Entering the cellar, he was relieved to know it would be the last time.

Hopefully I won't have to see you guys ever again, he thought as he crept among the skittering rats.

He smiled. After tonight, the rodents should be happy to have the cellar to themselves again.

As he crawled into the final tunnel, Rose could hear Hamilton a few feet behind him. They were going to be the first two men to escape. Each of the fifteen pairs of men had a copy of a map Robert Ford had given them, showing safe houses in the area. Still, what Rose was going to do once he was outside of the prison was the last thing on his mind. Being this close to freedom, he was even more anxious about getting caught than before.

Something's wrong, he thought, sweat dripping down his face as he scrambled through the tunnel. *Someone must have talked . . . Turner knows, the guards know . . . And they're going to be waiting for us on the other side of this tunnel! It's a trap, and I'll spend the rest of my days rotting in the darkness of the dungeon with the bugs and vermin . . .*

Rose squeezed through the tight sixteen-inch curve in the tunnel before scrambling upward. Thirty feet later he was in the tobacco shed, relieved to find it empty. The night air was cold, and felt good. Still, getting through the tunnel was only the beginning. Walking among the citizens and Confederate soldiers milling around town would be the true test of whether all their efforts had been worth it.

He waited a minute for Hamilton, who climbed up into the shed a few moments later. Both men brushed the dirt off their clothes and faces, then crept into the towing company office. Hamilton stopped at the office's front door and listened. Not hearing any footsteps, he slowly opened the door and the two men walked out of the shed and onto Canal Street. The street was empty save for one drunk man stumbling around. The Union officers paid him no mind and ambled out into the town.

They walked down the street with little fanfare. Then they turned a corner and, to their horror, found themselves on a block with a group of Confederate soldiers! The Rebs looked to be making the most of their night off, smoking and laughing outside of a saloon.

The former prisoners lowered their heads. They did their best not to walk too quickly.

"Hey you," a Southern voice called out as the

two escapees walked past.

Fear shot up their spines. Rose did his best to act unfazed as he stopped and turned around.

"You talkin' to me?" he said, putting on his best Southern accent.

"Yeah, I'm talkin' to you," the Reb said. He was wearing a guard's uniform. "I know you from somewhere?"

Rose shook his head. "I don't reckon you do, mister. I'm just passing through."

The guard had been leaning against a brick wall. Now he was moving toward them. "Naw, I knows you from someplace," he said, scratching his beard. "Where you from?"

"Biloxi."

"That right?"

Rose and Hamilton could tell the man wasn't buying it.

"Which regiment you serve with?"

"Fifty-Seventh."

"Where's your uniform, then? You know what—maybe you oughta come explain it to my commanding officer."

Rose glanced at Hamilton, who was trying his hardest not to panic. The colonel nodded to his old friend and smiled, silently bidding him farewell before turning back to the Confederate.

"I'll oblige you, sir, if it'll make you feel better."

"Yeah," the guard said. His breath reeked of alcohol. "It would."

The colonel briefly thought about making a run for it. But he kept his cool and went with the guard, who led him over to a group of men in neatly pressed Confederate uniforms. Knowing it was too risky to wait around, Hamilton disappeared into the shadows of a nearby alley.

"Got a man over here, sir," the suspicious guard said to his superior, nodding at Rose. "Says he's from Mississippi, but I don't believe him. Looks like a Yankee boy to me."

Rose wasn't sure if the man was harassing him for the fun of it or because of his disheveled, weakened appearance—a common look among Libby prisoners.

The commanding officer glanced at the clearly inebriated guard and scoffed.

"Have you got any evidence?"

"Just look at him . . . I'm tellin' you, he ain't no Reb like he claims."

Rose steeled himself as the Confederate in charge gave him a long, hard look.

Should I run? No, they'd shoot me . . . Rose felt paralyzed.

After what seemed like an eternity, the commanding officer turned back to the suspicious guard.

"Sleep it off, private," he said, then to Rose, "Go about your business."

Rose nodded. "Good night, gentlemen," he said. He then turned and walked away slowly. His heart felt like it was about to beat out of his chest.

As he continued along, Rose began to see a few more of his comrades walking slowly through the town square. They went unnoticed among the raucous Confederates.

He couldn't find Hamilton. That was okay, though—he didn't expect his trusted partner to stick around. It was every man for himself now.

Wanting to get as far away from Richmond as

he could, Rose headed for the city limits. He knew if he headed southeast through the swamps that he'd eventually make it to the Union outpost in Williamsburg. He hoped that this few hours' head start would be all he needed.

He rounded another corner. To his horror, there stood Warden Dick Turner, having a beer and a smoke with his cohorts. Rose kept walking, but he covered his face with his arm and pretended to cough into it.

"The major's convinced himself there's gonna be a big escape attempt soon," Turner said to his friends. "I told him he's mistaken. We've got them boys right where we want 'em."

Rose ducked into the first alley he could find and headed for the next street over. As he hurried along, he heard more voices behind him and what sounded like a confrontation.

It's only a matter of time now, he thought to himself, *before our ruse is discovered.*

Then he turned and headed for the city limits.

Chapter Ten

ON THE RUN

Splash!

Rose cursed as he trudged out of the freezing waters of the Chickahominy. He'd tripped in a hole while wading across the river, and his clothes were completely soaked.

The morning's first rays of sunlight shone through the foggy haze. Rose's wet boots squished as he stepped onto the riverbank. Up ahead were some woods. He headed toward them, his breath steaming in the frigid morning air.

Upon entering the forest, he leaned briefly against a large oak tree.

My feet are killing me. Couldn't hurt to rest for five minutes . . .

Shivering under his wet jacket, he sat down against the tree and closed his eyes.

Just a . . . few minutes, he thought. It wasn't long before he had drifted into sleep.

He suddenly jolted awake, his eyes wild. He could hear dogs barking, along with the sound of thundering hooves.

There was little doubt in his mind that it was a Rebel search party.

They've discovered our escape! Have to run . . . NOW!

Using every ounce of strength he had, Rose dashed through the woods. He was exhausted. Each step he took felt like there were ten-pound bricks in his boots. He hadn't gone far when he tripped on a log and toppled over. Rose staggered back to his feet. On pure adrenaline, he forced himself to keep moving. The horses and the dogs were getting closer. He could hear men shouting, but he dared not turn to see how far they were. He just kept running.

The colonel reached a ditch overgrown with a thick canopy of thorn-covered vines. He fell to the ground and began crawling on his belly into the ditch, the tangled nest of thorns ripping his uniform and flesh. But he kept going, only stopping to lie still when he heard the horses stop close by.

"I saw him!" Rose heard one of the men say over the barking dogs. "I know I saw that Yank runnin'!"

"He couldn't have gotten far," another man said.

The longest minute of Rose's life passed. He breathed a sigh of relief when he heard the men ride on. As much as it hurt, he crawled his way out of the thorns as fast as he could. Then he continued his run.

Five days after he'd escaped from Libby, Colonel Rose stepped out into an open field. As if looking at a mirage, he couldn't believe what he was seeing. A few hundred yards away, he spotted a small group of soldiers on horseback—and they were wearing blue Union jackets.

I made it! I finally made it!

"Hey!" he shouted. "Over here!"

Wobbling on weak, shaky legs, he started

toward them. They saw him and began riding over. As the men got closer, Rose's smile faded. He'd made a mistake. These men weren't Union soldiers—they were Confederates in blue jackets! And one of them was Dick Turner!

Rose turned to run, but he was too weak. One of the Rebs leaped from his horse and tackled him to the ground. Rose struggled, but soon a second

soldier was on top of him.

The men wrestled Rose to his feet. He found himself face-to-face with the sneering Turner.

"We caught you, boy," the warden growled. Rose's face twisted at the smell of his rancid breath. "All your work was for nothing. And I's gonna see to it personal that—"

All of Rose's rage suddenly boiled to the surface. With his last burst of strength, he broke free and snatched a rifle away from one of the men. Then he hit Turner across the face with it.

The warden grunted and fell to the ground.

Rose turned and ran. He didn't get far, however, before he was tackled again. The Confederates surrounded him.

As he lay on the ground, Turner reappeared. He was bleeding and angry.

"You dirty Yank . . ."

Turner kicked him in the face. Then the other soldiers joined in. By the time he began the long march back to Libby, Rose was badly beaten.

Two days after Rose was captured, Hamilton arrived at the Union lines outside Williamsburg.

He'd decided to travel through the thick swamps where no Rebs on horseback were crazy enough to go. Half frozen and cut to shreds by the thorns, the major staggered into the Union camp.

A crowd of stunned bluecoats turned and watched in silence as he approached them.

"My name's Andrew Hamilton," he told them, identifying himself. "Major. Twelfth Kentucky Cavalry. I've just escaped from Libby Prison."

Colonel Rose followed the Rebel guard down the creaky wooden steps and into the dark bowels of the Libby Prison dungeon. Candle in hand, the guard opened one of the steel doors and shoved Rose inside.

"Let's see you dig your way outa there, boy!" the guard cackled.

The cell was packed with prisoners, the other men groaning at the prospect of less space. Rose caught glimpses of their skeletal faces, a sea of ghostly eyes staring back at him in the darkness. There was hardly any room to sit, let alone lie down. Not that Rose would want to lie down. He could already feel the rats scurrying over his boots. The smell of waste was almost overwhelming, and he could make out a filthy toilet in the middle of the cell.

The guard went back upstairs, taking the light with him. Rose closed his eyes and hung his head.

For a while, I was free, he told himself. *I escaped. They can't take that away from me.*

"Colonel Rose?" a voice called from somewhere in the dark. "That you?"

"I'm afraid so," Rose replied.

"Maybe I shouldn't have pulled you out of that chimney after all," the man said.

Rose recognized the voice.

"Bennett!"

The two friends embraced. The others in the dungeon listened, grateful for the entertainment, as Bennett started to describe the scene after Rose and Hamilton had departed Libby.

"It was a mess, Colonel," he said. "I was on the last shift out. The word soon got out to all the prisoners about the tunnel. There was a mad dash for the fireplace. It was a regular stampede. Men were starting to fight over who got to go next. Finally, everyone ran back upstairs once they heard one of the guards outside the window. We all thought the jig was up.

"I went back a half hour later," he continued. "There was no crowd there this time. Guess everyone realized nobody would get out if they made too much racket. Anyway, I made it to the cellar and crawled into the tunnel. When I got to the narrowest passage—where the tunnel gets real small—I found myself face-to-face with a pair of legs kicking every which way. They belonged to Colonel Streight. The old boy was stuck and frightened as all get out."

Rose had to chuckle. Colonel Abel Streight, infamous for his raids on Alabama and Mississippi, was almost as well-known for his large girth. He was one of the heaviest of Libby's inmates—a true feat considering the lack of food.

"I managed to talk him down and helped pull him out by the boots," the prisoner recounted. "Once I got the colonel out, he stripped down to his underwear. Carrying his clothes, the colonel was able to squeeze through, but just barely!"

"I'm sorry to see you were captured. How'd it happen?"

"They found me in the woods just north of Richmond," Bennett said.

"Last I heard, they caught about forty of us. Two men drowned trying to swim across the river. Reckon we're luckier than they are."

"I reckon you're right," Rose said. "It's good to see you, Bennett."

Over the next two months, Rose managed to survive on what little corn bread and water the guards gave him. He and Bennett also ate the occasional rat they caught, cooking with matches handed down through the floorboards from charitable prisoners in the rooms above.

Sleeping was more difficult. Rose tried to find space on the wall to lean against, resting in snatches. On more than one occasion he fell to the floor, where rats and spiders bit his flesh.

Time passed. Rose didn't know how much, as there were no windows in the dungeon to tell day from night.

April arrived. Rose was feeling around the floor, looking for a rat to catch for dinner, when the door opened. A guard stood in the doorway, holding a candle.

"Rose! Bennett!" the guard said, before naming three others. "Move it out!"

The five prisoners were led up the stairs, back onto the main floor of the prison. They were then taken outside into the sunlight. Rose and Bennett, with their long, stringy beards and filthy uniforms, shielded their eyes.

"Into the carriage, boys," the guard said. "Y'all are going back North. Prisoner exchange."

Rose's dry, cracked lips broke into a grin.

I can't believe it, he thought, feeling the warmth of the sun for the first time in months. Seven months after entering Libby Prison and two months after his escape attempt, he was finally free.

EPILOGUE

On the night of the Libby Prison escape, 109 of the 1,200 prisoners made it out. Of those, 59 managed to evade recapture and make it to safety. The prison break remains one of the most successful and ingenious wartime escapes of all time.

Robert E. Lee, the general of the Confederacy, surrendered his army at Appomattox on April 9, 1865. The North simply had too many resources at their disposal, and the South was outmanned and outgunned. By the end of the war, many of the Confederate troops were underfed and in tattered clothes. The Civil War was officially over. The North had won.

Robert Ford managed to escape Libby in 1864 after surviving a punishment of five hundred lashes ordered by Dick Turner. Ford got a job in the US treasury department, where he worked until his death five years later, which many attributed to internal injuries from the lashing.

Confederate troops abandoned Richmond, setting fire to the city on their way out. As Richmond burned, one man remained at Libby Prison—Major Thomas Turner. He torched any documents that could incriminate him for his treatment of Union soldiers, then—realizing that Union troops would be out for vengeance—he fled the country. First he went to Cuba, then Canada. Thomas Turner died in 1901.

Warden Dick Turner, on the other hand, wasn't so lucky. He was caught by Union troops as he tried to escape. One of the men in the squad who captured him had spent time in Libby.

"I think I have a good idea where we can keep this dog," the Union soldier said. "Let's put him up in Libby's dungeon."

"No!" Turner screamed. He begged and pleaded, but nobody listened.

Warden Turner actually managed to escape the hell he had left so many men to rot in. With a smuggled knife, he carved through the few wooden bars that hadn't been replaced with iron and ran off into the night. He was recaptured soon after, however, and scheduled for execution. Ultimately, Libby's old warden was saved when Thomas Turner managed to torch the files that would have incriminated them both for war crimes. Like his former boss, Dick Turner also died in 1901.

Many in the Union wanted to burn Libby to the ground, but for the next thirty or so years, the prison was kept as a landmark. In 1889, it was dismantled and rebuilt in Chicago as a museum. Major Hamilton was one of its first visitors. Then in 1899, it was dismantled for the final time and its bricks and timbers were sold off as building materials. It's believed to survive in barns and other structures around Illinois to this day.

After the war, Major Andrew G. Hamilton penned an account of the escape that was widely published and could be bought for a dime (as what was known at the time as a "dime store novel") at the Libby Prison Museum in Chicago. Hamilton died in 1895 when he was shot and killed in an argument with another man near Morgantown, West Virginia.

After regaining his health, Rose continued to fight for the Union, serving in the Atlanta campaign. Once the war ended in 1865, he elected to stay in the regular army, where he served until retiring in 1894. Despite his fame as the mastermind of the Libby Prison escape, Rose didn't like to speak about the breakout. He died in 1907 at the age of seventy-seven. Part of his gravestone reads: "Engineered and Executed the Libby Prison Tunnel."

AUTHOR'S NOTE

In order to streamline the story and heighten the drama, I've taken a few liberties with the timeline and events. Liberties were also taken with timing of the day and night shifts to heighten suspense and improve pacing. Warden Dick Turner, for example, was not the Confederate that Colonel Rose hit with the rifle prior to his recapture, nor was he present at the scene—I wanted our story's hero to confront the villain. Rose and Hamilton actually met for the first time in "Rat Hell," aka the east cellar, when it was a temporary kitchen and prisoners were allowed access. However, it was soon sealed off by the guards; hence Rose and Bennett had to go in through the fireplace. And as for the colonel's old friend Bennett, though the latter was recaptured, their meeting in the depths of Libby's infamous dungeon is fictitious (though it could've happened). Certain character traits and dialogue were also fictionalized, but all the men named were real. For further reading about this great escape I highly recommend the excellent *Libby Prison Breakout* by Joseph Wheelan, which was the main source for this book.

SELECTED BIBLIOGRAPHY

Beard, Rick. "The Great Civil War Escape." *New York Times*, February 11, 2014.

Boaz, Thomas M. *Libby Prison and Beyond: A Union Staff Officer in the East, 1862–1865*. Shippensburg, PA: Burd Street Press, 1999.

Brooks, Rebecca Beatrice. "Elizabeth Van Lew: Spymaster." Civil War Saga. November 9, 2012. http:// civilwarsaga.com/elizabeth-van-lew-spymaster/.

Brown, Jim. "Lice and the American Civil War Soldier." Gazkhan's Re-enacting, History and Hobbies Page. Last accessed May 18, 2019. http:// home.freeuk.com/gazkhan/lice.htm.

Cable, G. W. (editor) *Famous Adventures and Prison Escapes of the Civil War*. New York: The Century Co., 1913.

Hamilton, Andrew G. *Story of the Famous Tunnel Escape from Libby Prison*. Chicago: Libby Prison War Museum Association, 1893. Published online February 8, 2015. https://civilwarrichmond .com/prisons/libby-prison/4459-1893-hamilton -andrew-g-story-of-the-famous-tunnel-escape -from-libby-prison-excellent-published-account

-regarding-the-tunnel-escape-from-libby-prison
-one-of-the-most-reliable-sources.

Herrin, Dean. "The Great Escape." Discover the
Story. Crossroads of War. Last accessed May 18,
2019. http://www.crossroadsofwar.org/discover
-the-story/african-americans-the-struggle-for
-freedom/african-americans-the-struggle-for
-freedom/.

Miller, Gary L. "Historical Natural History: Insects
and the Civil War." Entomology Group. Montana
State University. Last accessed May 18, 2019.
http://www.montana.edu/historybug/civilwar2/.

Wheelan, Joseph. *Libby Prison Breakout*. New York:
Public Affairs Books, 2010.

ABOUT THE AUTHOR

W. N. BROWN is a writer and journalist from Henderson, Texas. In addition to authoring *Civil War Breakout*, he has written for Time-Life Books' *Mysteries of the Unknown* and *Mysteries of the Criminal Mind*, and written articles on historical artifacts, scientific discoveries, and popular culture for *Men's Journal*, *Fox News*, and *Maxim*. He lives in New York City.

ABOUT THE SERIES EDITOR

MICHAEL TEITELBAUM has been a writer and editor of children's books for more than twenty-five years. He worked on staff as an editor at Golden Books, Grossett & Dunlap, and Macmillan. As a writer, Michael's fiction work includes *The Scary States of America*, fifty short stories—one from each state—all about the paranormal, published by Random House; and *The Very Hungry Zombie: A Parody*, done with artist extraordinaire Jon Apple, published by Skyhorse. His nonfiction work includes *Jackie Robinson: Champion for Equality*, published by Sterling; *The Baseball Hall of Fame*, a two-volume encyclopedia, published by Grolier; *Sports in America, 1980–89*, published by Chelsea House; and *Great Moments in Women's Sports* and *Great Inventions: Radio and Television*, both published by World Almanac Library. Michael lives with his wife, Sheleigah, and two talkative cats in the beautiful Catskill Mountains of upstate New York, where he and Sheleigah also host a music program on WIOX Community Radio.

Turn the page for a sneak peek at the next
DEATH-DEFYING GREAT ESCAPE!

Chapter One

A FATEFUL DECISION
MONDAY, DECEMBER 13, 1920

"Beautiful view from up here," murmured navy lieutenant Walter Hinton as he looked down from the wicker basket that hung beneath the gas balloon. "But it's a long way down!"

Two thousand feet below lay the Brooklyn Navy Yard. The ships just off the coast looked like toys in a bathtub. Hinton gazed in wonder at small buildings, tiny roads, and people the size of ants. The entire world stretched out in miniature beneath him.

"Don't lean so far over the side," cautioned Lieutenant Louis Kloor, only half seriously. "We wouldn't want to lose you this early in our flight."

Kloor, the leader of this training flight across

New York state, smiled. At age twenty-two he was ten years younger than Hinton and young enough to be the son of forty-five-year-old Lieutenant Stephen Farrell, the third member of their team. Hinton and Farrell, both good friends of Kloor's, were on board because the navy wanted all its officers to have some balloon experience. The two older men called blue-eyed, smooth-faced Kloor "The Kid," but despite his youth, Kloor was a seasoned ballooning veteran.

THREE MEN OF ACTION

Hinton and Farrell may not have been experienced balloonists, but they were veteran airplane pilots.

Hinton grew up on a farm in Ohio and joined the navy as a young man. In May 1919, he was one of two pilots in a six-man crew that flew the NC-4, a pioneering four-engine airplane, across the Atlantic Ocean. The NC-4 was the only one of the three airplanes in the flight to succeed. The other two were forced to land in the ocean due to poor visibility. But Hinton's NC-4 carried on, arriving in Lisbon, Portugal, after a nineteen-day flight. They were the first aviators to cross the Atlantic, eight years before Charles Lindbergh's celebrated transatlantic solo flight. Hinton was awarded the Navy Cross and a Congressional Gold Medal for his achievement.

Farrell was born near Oswego, New York, and enlisted in the navy in 1896. In World War I he was an armament officer at a US naval air station in England. In his younger days, Farrell was a first-class boxer and attained the title of heavyweight champion of the Pacific Fleet, a title he defended for years. Now, at age forty-five, he weighed two hundred pounds and struggled to keep his weight down with exercise and diet.

Kloor, despite his youth, had his own list of achievements. A native of Louisiana, he was one of the youngest aviators in the US Navy and had already flown ten balloon trips. He'd also seen his share of danger. In 1918, a balloon he was flying snagged on a tree over Milford, Connecticut, and was destroyed. Then in July 1920, only five months before his flight with Hinton and Farrell, Kloor had survived a crash over Jamaica Bay, New York, when his navy dirigible, a gas-filled airship, crashed into the sea. Kloor was well aware of the risks of flying, but on the morning of December 13 he had no reason to believe the training flight across New York state would be anything but routine.

About two hours into the flight from the Rockaway Naval Air Station at the westward end of Long Island, Kloor took out a sheet of paper and began writing.

"What are you doing?" Farrell asked.

"I'm writing down our coordinates for the naval officials back at Rockaway to let them know our position," he explained. Then he opened the birdcage attached to the rigging and carefully lifted out one of the four carrier pigeons with both hands. He attached the note to the bird's leg and gently let it go. The pigeon flapped its wings and took off for home.

"Smart bird," said Hinton.

"The smartest," agreed Kloor. "It'll get our message back to the station.."

Lieutenant Farrell looked at the bird as it slowly grew smaller, until it became no more than a dot in the sea of sky. Then he stared down at the earth far below. He was both fascinated by and fearful of the balloon.

Unlike an airplane, it had no engine and no mechanism to steer. It was the hydrogen gas that allowed it to soar in the skies. The pilot could only control it going up or down. To go up, he had to pour out sand from one of the twenty-one thirty-pound sandbags in the basket, lightening the load. This was the ballast. To descend, the pilot opened a valve to release some of the hydrogen gas.

CARRIER PIGEONS

For more than three thousand years, carrier pigeons have been able to find their homes over long distances, using "compass sense," which allows the birds to orient themselves by the sun, allowing them to deliver written messages. The ancient Egyptians were among the first people to keep carrier pigeons.

In 1860, newsman Paul Reuter, who would go on to start a news wire service, developed a fleet of forty-five pigeons to deliver news and stock reports between Brussels, Belgium, and Aachen, Germany.

Carrier pigeons were also used in the Franco-Prussian War (1870–71) to deliver messages. Pigeons were released from balloons hovering over the city. Pigeons were used in even greater numbers during World War I. One particularly heroic French pigeon, named Cher Ami, was awarded the Croix de Guerre (War Cross) for delivering twelve important messages. On his final mission, he survived being shot through the breast and leg.

The United States Signal Corps used carrier pigeons to send messages in World War II (1939–45) and in the Korean War (1950–53).

Today, carrier pigeons, more often called homing pigeons, are mostly kept for racing. The birds are let go at a release point by each owner. The bird arriving back at its home loft in the fastest time is the winner. However, in a remote part of eastern India, police were using pigeons to communicate with victims of natural disasters as late as 2002.

♦♦♦

The three men passed a pleasant afternoon in comfortable chairs in the balloon's basket as they crossed the state of New York in a northerly direction. Although it was cold, they stayed warm in their bulky flight suits, which were lined with silk, insulated with a layer of fleece, and overlaid with a tightly woven, weatherproof cotton.

"Sorry to be so last-minute in inviting you on the flight," said Kloor, as he bit into one of the eight sandwiches they had packed.

"It's all right," said Farrell, sipping hot coffee from a thermos bottle. "I needed to get away and get my mind off Sis."

"I didn't know you had a sister," said Hinton.

"Oh, no," laughed Farrell. "Sis is what I call my daughter Emily. She's ill at home in Ridgewood, New Jersey, with scarlet fever. But I hope to cheer her up with stories about our balloon adventure when we get back."

The night slowly descended like a thick curtain and they gazed up at the stars beginning to appear in the darkened sky, sparkling like salt crystals.

"It's beautiful," murmured Farrell. "Thanks

again for inviting me along."

"You would have had to go up sooner or later," Kloor said to Farrell.

"Well, I'm glad it's sooner than later," said Hinton, taking another sip of the hot coffee. It warmed his body as the night air grew colder.

"What's that down there?" asked Kloor, scanning the ground below. "Looks like a light coming from a house."

"You've got a good pair of eyes," said Farrell, squinting into the darkness. "I never would have spotted it."

"Well, gentlemen," said Kloor, "I think it's time we found out what our position is."

He opened the valve and released some of the gas. The balloon began a slow descent through the deepening darkness. Suddenly, the drag rope trailing outside the balloon pulled tight, getting caught in a tangle of tree branches. The balloon came to a stop about a hundred feet from the ground.

"Not to worry," said Kloor calmly. "We can get the rope untangled once we find out where we are."

Through the trees, they saw the house again,

more clearly now. A man emerged from within.

"Excuse me, sir!" Kloor yelled down to him. "Can you tell us where we are?"

The man was startled by the balloon hovering above his home, but soon regained his composure. "You're near the town of Wells," he cried. "In the Adirondacks."

"And how far are we from Albany?" asked Kloor, referring to the state capital.

The man raised one arm and pointed to the southeast. "About sixty miles thata way," he said.

Kloor thanked him and turned to his two companions. "Well, gentlemen, if you've had enough, this could be the end of our voyage. We could land the balloon safely right here, walk into town, and make our way home in the morning," he told them.

Farrell and Hinton exchanged looks.

"Is that normal for a training flight?" Hinton asked.

"Well, no," replied Kloor. "They normally last a full twenty-four hours, meaning we would be landing tomorrow."

"Then I'm for going on," said Hinton.

"I agree," said Farrell.

Ready For More Risks?
Read the GREAT ESCAPES series!